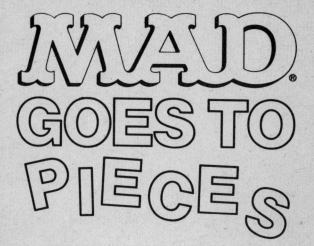

MAD. GOES TO PIECEs

FRANK JACOBS

WARNER BOOKS

A Warner Communications Company

WARNER BOOKS EDITION

Copyright © 1984 by Frank Jacobs and E.C. Publications, Inc.
All rights reserved.
No part of this book may be reproduced without permission.
For information address:
E.C. Publications, Inc.
485 Madison Avenue
New York, N.Y. 10022

Title "MAD" used with permission of its owner,
E.C. Publications, Inc.

This Warner Books Edition is published by arrangement with
E.C. Publications, Inc.

Designed by Tom Nozkowski

Warner Books, Inc.
666 Fifth Avenue
New York, N.Y. 10103

Ⓦ A Warner Communications Company

Printed in the United States of America

First Warner Books Printing: July, 1984

10 9 8 7 6 5 4 3 2 1

FOREWORD
by Nick Meglin

Because Frank Jacobs is an active member of "Born Again Born Again," an exclusive cult of re-incarnates who remember former lives, he often confuses his present and past, thus forgetting in which era he now exists. For example, last Tuesday we were having lunch and Frank, a name-dropper of the highest order, mentioned that it was he and not Eugene O'Neill that helped Charles Lamb write Shakespeare's plays.

"Frank," I said, "the belief is that it was **Bacon** who wrote some works generally attributed to Shakespeare."

"Bacon? Lamb? I thought I ordered **duck!**"

"Frank," I said, "you ordered **veal!** Not to mention that Eugene O'Neill lived in the 20th century and therefore couldn't have ... "

"Not **that** Eugene O'Neill," interrupted Frank, "the guy I'm talking about used to get together with me and Chaucer when we kidded Balzac about his **'Decameron'**".

"You mean **'Droll Stories,'**" I said.

"They sure were! That Bernie Shaw could teach Tolstoy a few things about writing TV sit-coms!"

All this serves only to make the reader of this book aware of what the problem is—namely, that Frank Jacobs believes these ancient prints are contemporary works, and that the clever dialogue he has provided is ancient prose. Who are we to destroy his past-present little world with ridiculous abstractions like **fact, logic,** and **truth?** After all, he may be right. For as Socrates said ... or was it Neil Simon ..?

Business

As

Usual

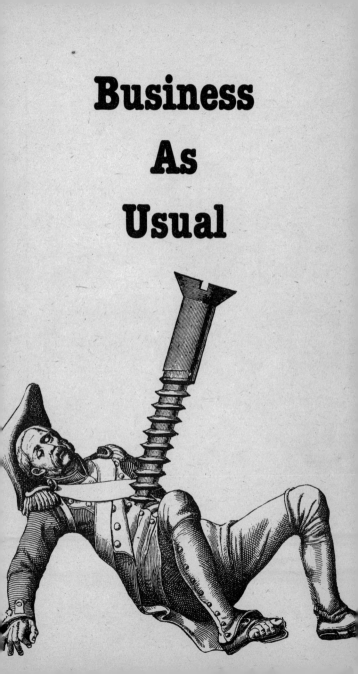

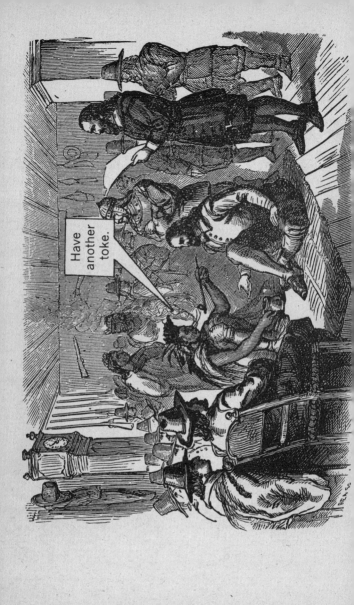

Great Moments in World Commerce

New Guinea Opens Its B

rders to Foreign Investors

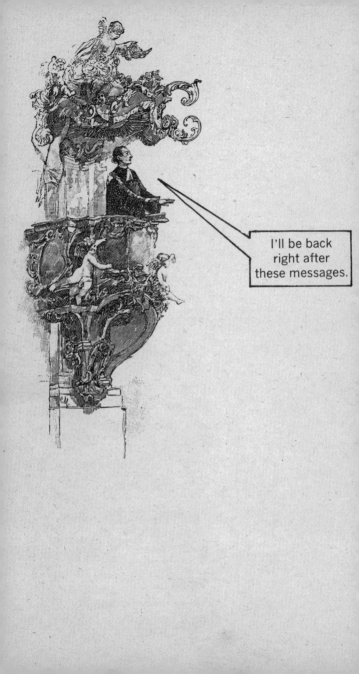

The
Facts
of
Life

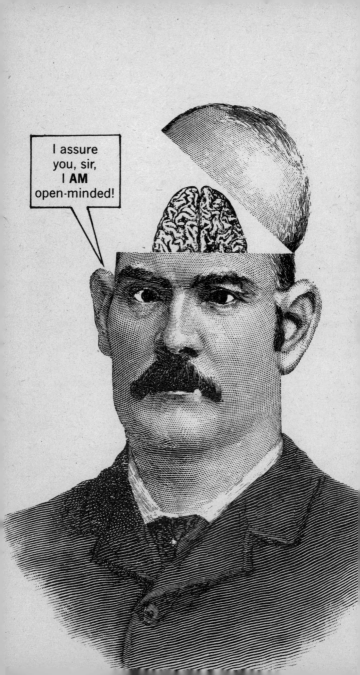

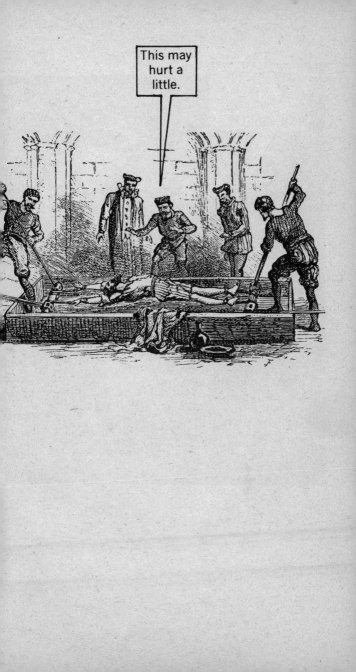

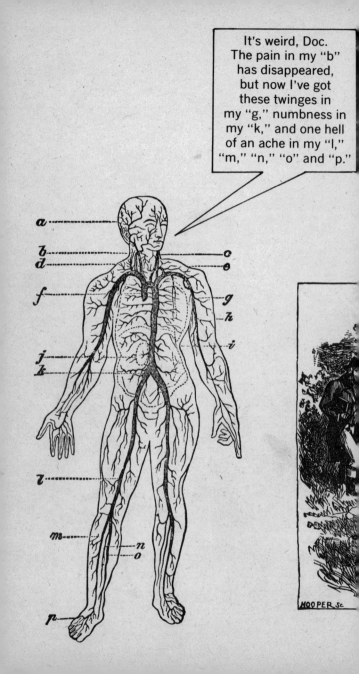

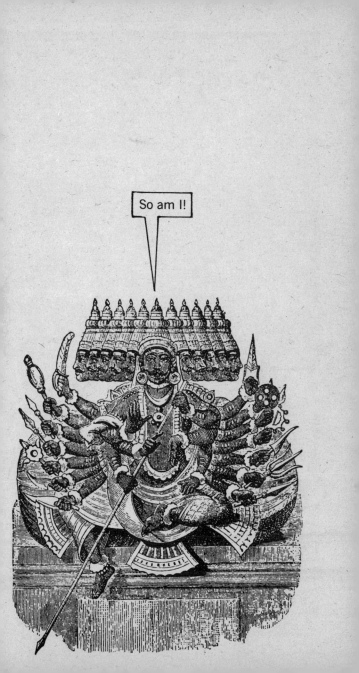

The
Great
Outdoors

CUT! Larry, when I asked you to play Washington straight, I didn't mean you should make him a stiff! Ralph, you're holding the flag like a sack of flour! It's the symbol of America, for Chrissake! And you rowers, you look like you're practicing for some friggin' regatta! Dammit, we're gonna do it again till we get it right—and I don't care if you all freeze your butts off!

Great
Moments
in
Sports

The First Running of the New York City Marathon

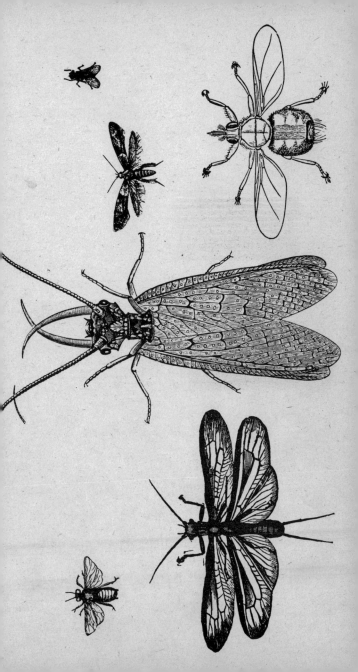

The
Upper
Crust

"...but Peter Cottontail saw the fox just in time and said as he scrambled down his rabbit-hole, 'You won't catch **me** this fine sunny morning!'"

And I **too** have enjoyed our I.R.S. audit, Mr. Conroy.

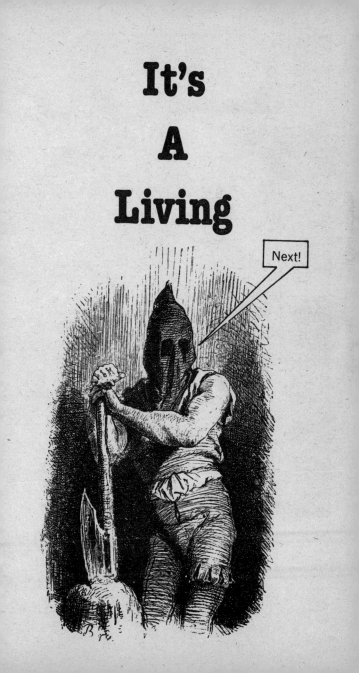

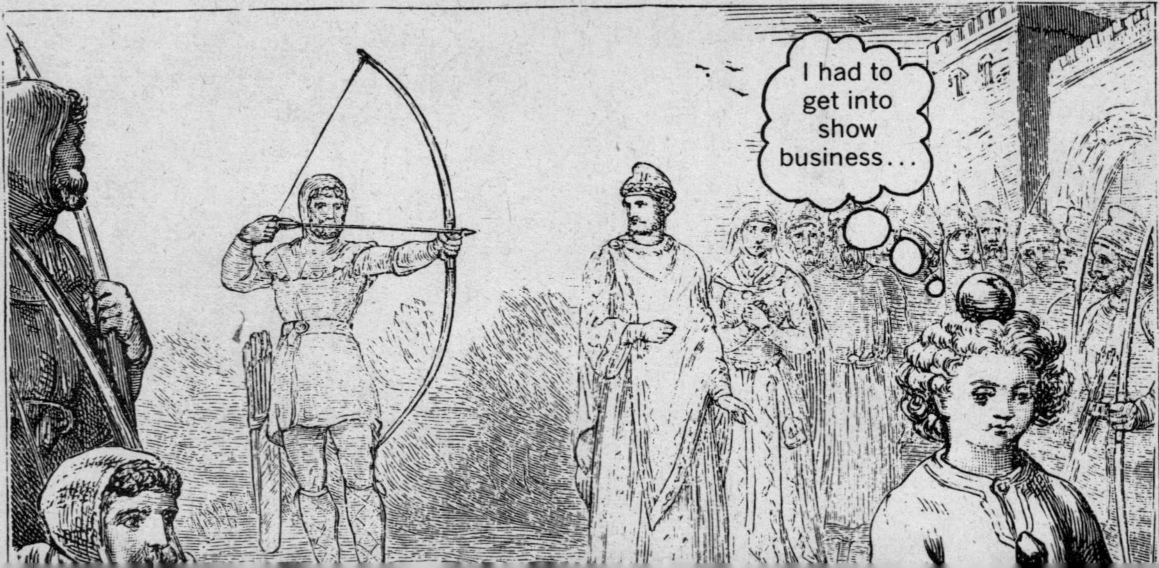
I had to get into show business...

Quoth the raven, "Not a chance!" That's not it. Quoth the raven, "Nosiree!" That's not it. Quoth the raven, "Hey, no way!" That's not it...

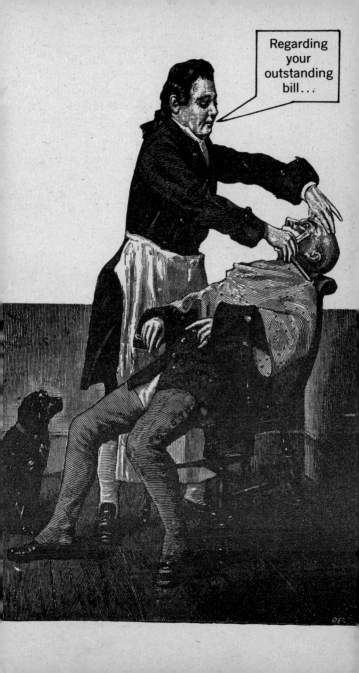

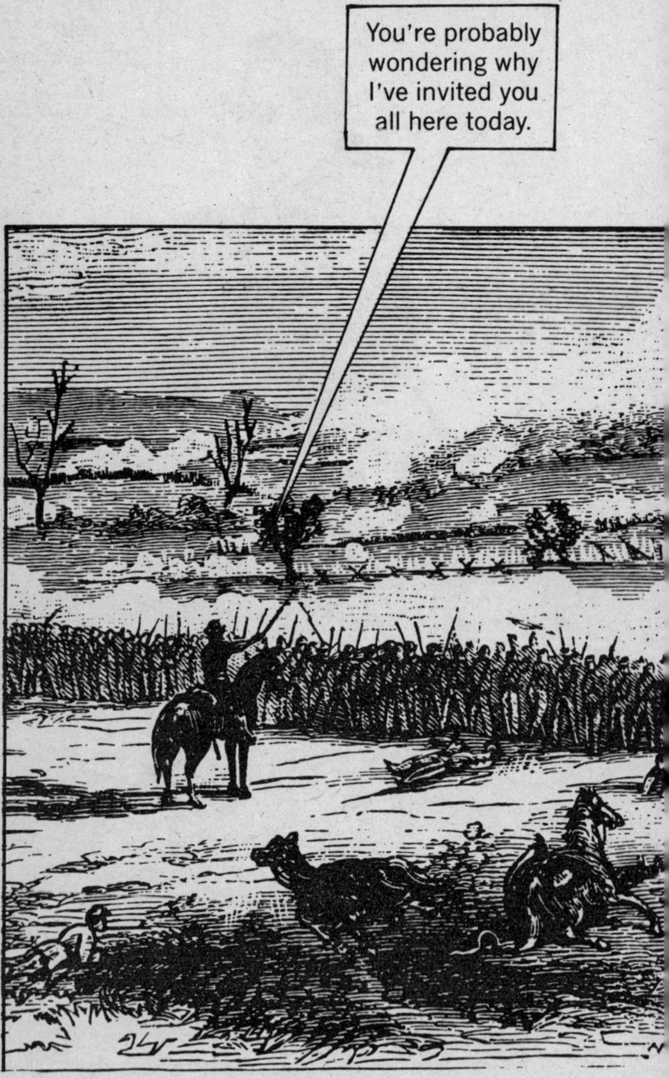
You're probably wondering why I've invited you all here today.

It's a simple question, Robert. The dealer is showing a 7. You've been dealt a 13. Do you stand or take a hit?

Going

Places

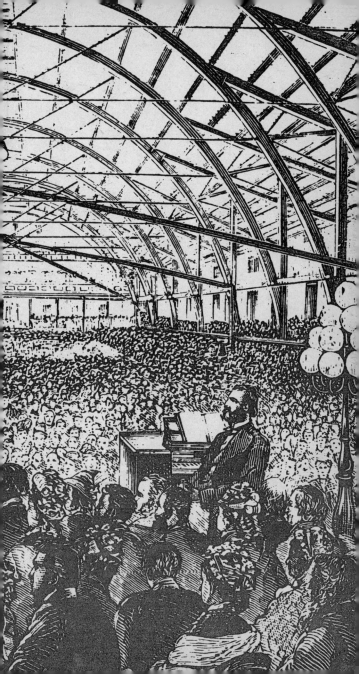

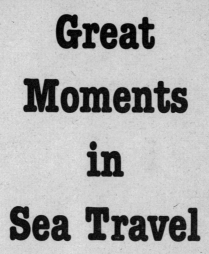

Great
Moments
in
Sea Travel

The Maiden Voyage of the Firs

Hydrogen-Fueled Steamship

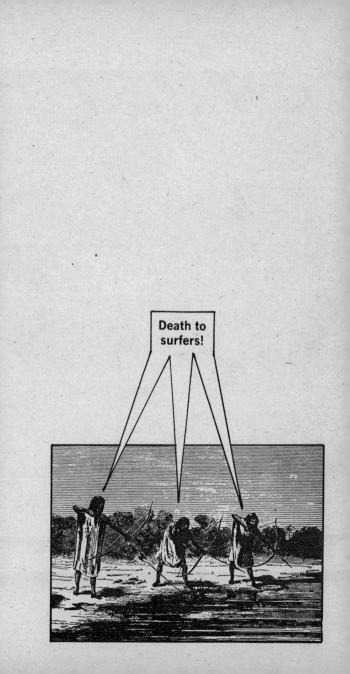

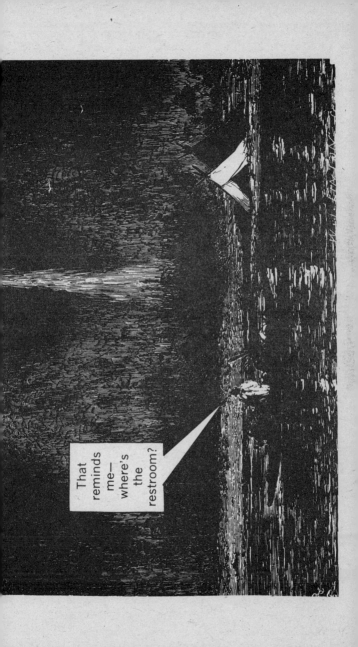

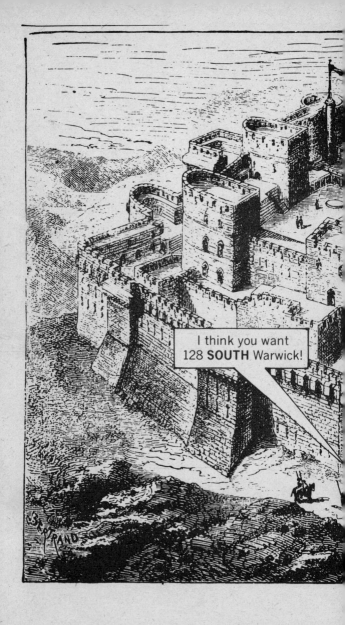

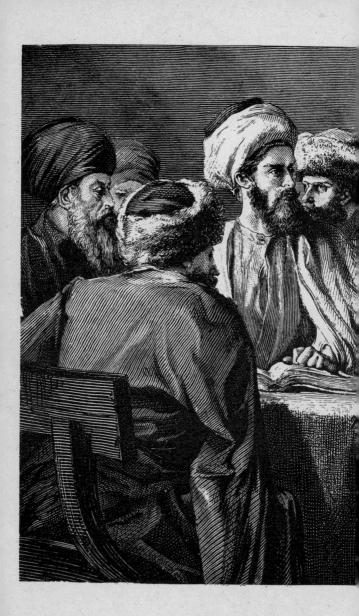

Then, with only seconds
left on the clock,
Bradshaw faked the hand-off
and faded back to pass!
H.U.

Getting
Carried
Away

So?

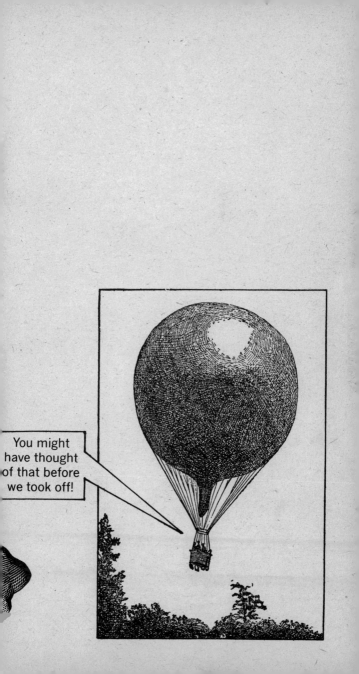

Parting
Shots

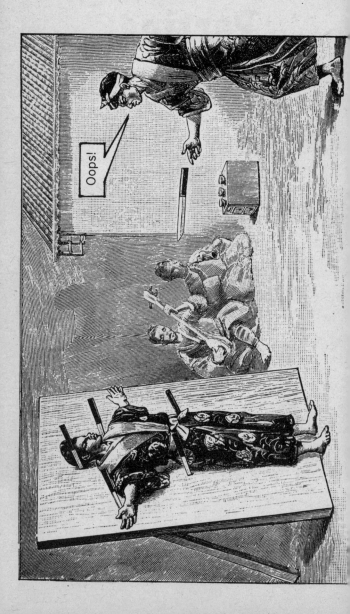

Great
Moments
in
Show
Business

The Morning After the F

al Concert of "The Who"

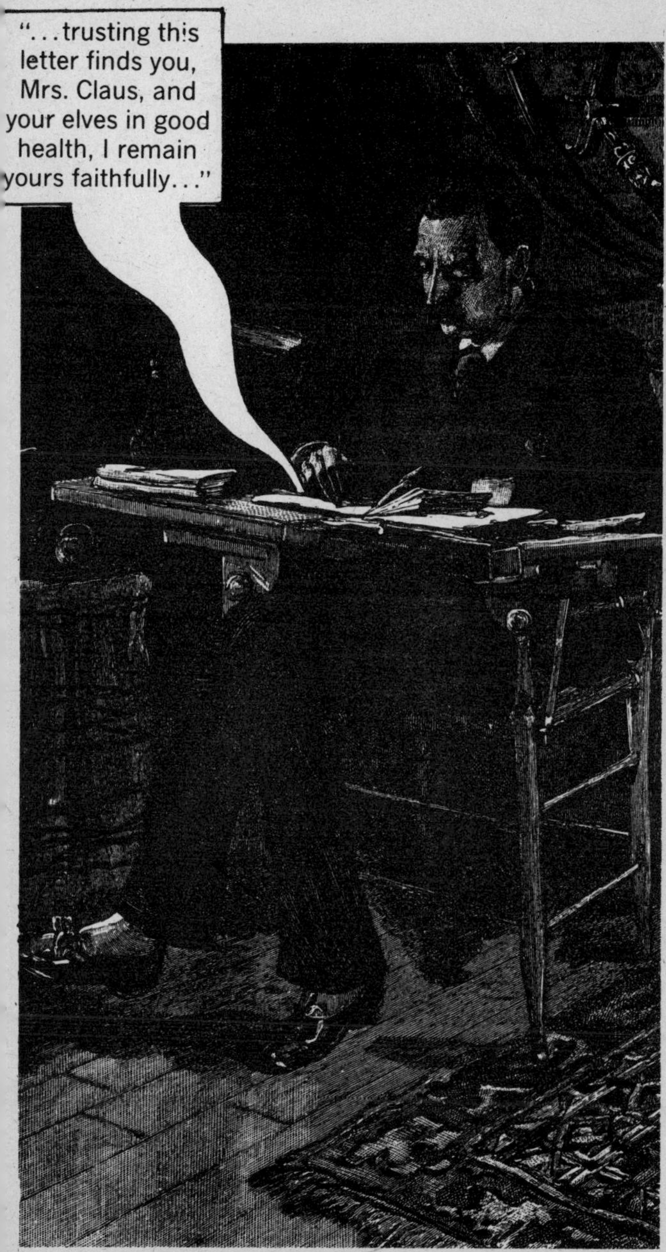
"...trusting this letter finds you, Mrs. Claus, and your elves in good health, I remain yours faithfully..."

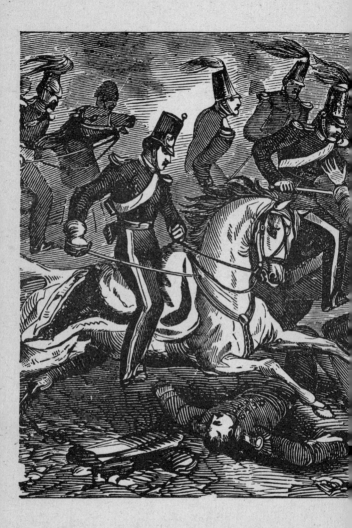

Some people will do anything to get their names in the Guinness Book of Records.

And now that you've finished **this** book, think of all the fun you'll have reading all of Frank Jacobs' **other** books, such as "Mad Goes Wild," "Mad About Sports," "Mad Around the World," "Mad's Talking Stamps," "More Mad About Sports," "Mad For Better or Verse," "Sing Along With Mad," "Get Stuffed With Mad," "The Mad Jumble Book," and "The Mad Jock Book!"